Merry Christmas, Peppa!

Adapted by Melanie McFadyen

This book is based on the TV series *Peppa Pig*. *Peppa Pig* is created by Neville Astley and Mark Baker.
Peppa Pig © Astley Baker Davies Ltd/Entertainment One UK Ltd 2003.

ISBN 978-1-338-57331-2

10 9 8 7 6 5 4 3 2 1   19 20 21 22 23
Printed in the U.S.A.   40

First printing 2019
Book design by Mercedes Padró and Marissa Asuncion

www.peppapig.com

SCHOLASTIC INC.

It is Christmas Day! Peppa and her family are opening their presents.

Peppa unwraps a toy car.
George unwraps a toy airplane.
"Hooray!" they cheer. "Vroooom!"
Daddy Pig reminds them to be careful when
playing.

But Peppa is too excited. She trips and bumps her arm. "Oww!" Peppa says. She's very hurt!

Thankfully, Mummy Pig knows just who to call—Doctor Brown Bear!

Doctor Brown Bear is sitting at his desk.

"A bumped arm, you say? And on Christmas Day? I'll be right there!" Doctor Brown Bear says.

Doctor Brown Bear arrives at Peppa's house.
"Can you wiggle your fingers?" he asks Peppa.
Peppa can!

"That's very good," Doctor Brown Bear says.
"But just to be safe, we'll take a trip to the
hospital."

At the hospital, Doctor Brown Bear takes Peppa to see Miss Rabbit. Miss Rabbit is the nurse.

Peppa looks around. She sees lots of Christmas decorations.

"Ooh, Miss Rabbit. The hospital is all Christmas-y!" Peppa says.
"Yes," Miss Rabbit replies. "Looks lovely, doesn't it?"

Miss Rabbit takes a picture of Peppa's arm with the X-ray. An X-ray shows her the bones inside Peppa's body.

"The X-ray shows your arm will be fine," Miss Rabbit announces. "And for being so brave, you get a sticker!"

"Hooray!" Peppa cheers. Peppa loves stickers!

Peppa walks out of Miss Rabbit's office. She sees a bed with Pedro Pony in it. Pedro Pony has bumped his leg. He has a sticker, too, but Pedro looks sad.

"I'm sad because Father Christmas hasn't come," says Pedro Pony.

Peppa is alarmed. That means Pedro hasn't gotten a Christmas present!

Then Peppa and Pedro hear
a voice in the hallway.
"Ho, ho, ho!" the voice
says. It's Father Christmas!

"I'm here with Pedro's Christmas present," Father Christmas says.

"Thank you, Father Christmas," Pedro
says. "I wonder what it is."
He unwraps the present. It's a toy boat!
Pedro loves his present.

"Sorry I'm a bit late. I got stuck in a
chimney." Father Christmas laughs. "Thank
you, Miss Rabbit, for looking after everyone at
Christmastime."

Peppa loves Christmas—even if it's at the hospital.
Merry Christmas!

Pedro Pony was very lucky that Father Christmas came to visit. But if Father Christmas hadn't come to visit, at least Pedro would have shared Christmas with Peppa!

Here are some ideas for you to spread Christmas cheer:

- Visit a friend, neighbor, or grandparent
- Decorate holiday cards or draw pictures for kids at the hospital
- Donate old toys
- Donate old books
- Bake cookies or cupcakes and donate them
- Sing a Christmas song for someone in need